For your mom. And mine. —S.L.

Mine too. —M.L.

Text copyright © 2025 by Suzanne Lang
Cover art and interior illustrations copyright © 2025 by Max Lang

Visit us on the Web! rhcbooks.com

Educators and librarians, for a variety of teaching tools, visit us at RHTeachersLibrarians.com

Library of Congress Cataloging-in-Publication Data
Names: Lang, Suzanne, author. | Lang, Max, illustrator. • Title: Grumpy monkey: mom for a day / Suzanne Lang; [illustrated by] Max Lang. • Other titles: Mom for a day • Description: First edition. | New York: Random House Studio, 2025. | Audience: Ages 4–8. | Summary: "Grumpy Monkey offers to babysit the little animals in the jungle, but when things go haywire, help comes from an unexpected source. Includes two pages of stickers."—Provided by publisher. • Identifiers: LCCN 2024019984 (print) | LCCN 2024019985 (ebook) | ISBN 978-0-593-70931-3 (hardcover) | ISBN 978-0-593-70932-0 (library binding) | ISBN 978-0-593-70933-7 (ebook) • Subjects: CYAC: Chimpanzees—Fiction. | Babysitters and Babysitting—Fiction. | Jungle animals—Fiction. | LCGFT: Animal fiction. | Picture books. Classification: LCC PZ7.1.L3437 Grut 2025 (print) | LCC PZ7.1.L3437 (ebook) | DDC [E]—dc23

The text of this book is set in 18-point Bernhard Gothic.
Book design by Nicole Gastonguay

MANUFACTURED IN CHINA
10 9 8 7 6 5 4 3 2 1
First Edition

GRUMPY MONKEY
MOM FOR A DAY

By Suzanne Lang

Illustrated by Max Lang

RANDOM HOUSE STUDIO
NEW YORK

One fine day, Jim Panzee and his neighbor Norman were splashing at the watering hole when Crocodile popped up, looking tired.

"Are you okay?" Jim asked.

"I am so tired," said Crocodile. "I wish I could take a nap, but my babies just want to splash and play." Crocodile yawned.

"We can play with your babies so you can take
a nap," said Jim. "We'll be their mom for the day."
"Slow down there, buddy," said Norman.
"I'd rather get in on that nap."

"Then I'll do it myself," said Jim.
"Being a mom is easy."

And it was fun, too.
The baby crocodiles liked
splashing as much as Jim.

Then Oxpecker came by. "Are you really being a mom for the day?" she asked.

"Yes," said Jim. "Being a mom is fun and easy."

"Great!" said Oxpecker. "Then you won't mind one more baby."

"Make that two," said Turtle.

"What about our babies?" said the other mothers. It was a lot of babies, but Jim didn't mind.

"Play with us, Mommy," the babies said. Jim played with the babies.

"We're tired, Mommy," the babies said. Jim took a nap with the babies.

I'm a great mom, Jim thought.

Jim wondered what would be fun to do
next with the babies. "How about a story?"
he suggested.

"Hooray!" said the babies.

"Once upon a time . . . ," Jim began.

But the babies weren't listening.

"I want to climb a tree."

"That was my idea!"

"I'm hungry!"

"I want to
hear the story!"

"This story stinks!"

Jim tried to tend to all the babies.

He picked up Baby Oxpecker and found
food for the hungry babies, but not all the
babies liked to eat the same things.

He did his best to keep the babies out of the trees so they wouldn't fall, but every time he got one baby out, another one would start to climb.

He made up a new story, and when
the babies didn't like that one, he made
up another and another. And then he told
the first story again.

He found flowers so that everyone would have one.

"No fair, Mommy," said Baby Otter. "Lion Cub's flower is bigger than mine."

"*Waaa,* we want big flowers, too," cried the others.

He got Baby Turtle unstuck from the rocks,
but then she got herself stuck in a bush.

He helped one baby snake with her old skin,
but then her brothers and sisters started molting, too.

All the while, the other babies were still hungry and climbing and arguing and getting stuck and asking to be carried and complaining and crying!

Finally, Jim couldn't take it anymore.

And he stormed off.

But just as quickly, he came rushing back.
"I can't leave you babies on your own."
Jim sighed.

And just as he was starting to feel really overwhelmed . . .

. . . his mom swung down from a tree and
picked him up. She calmed the babies and called
the other mothers and made everything all right.

"There should be a special day to celebrate moms," Jim said. "Because being a mom can be fun, but it is not easy."

"Every day is a great day to celebrate your mom," said Norman. Jim agreed.

And he gave his mom a big hug.